Littlest Pet Shop ™

THE ULTIMATE HANDBOOK

By Samantha Brooke

SCHOLASTIC INC.

New York   Toronto   London   Auckland   Sydney
Mexico City   New Delhi   Hong Kong   Buenos Aires

ISBN 0-439-88782-8

Littlest Pet Shop © 2006 Hasbro.
LITTLEST PET SHOP and all related characters
and elements are trademarks of and © Hasbro.
All Rights Reserved.

Published by Scholastic Inc. under license from HASBRO.
SCHOLASTIC and associated logos are trademarks
and/or registered trademarks of Scholastic Inc.

12 11 10 9 8 7 6 5 4 3 2 1   6 7 8 9 10/0

Book design by Two Red Shoes Design

Printed in the U.S.A.
First printing, September 2006

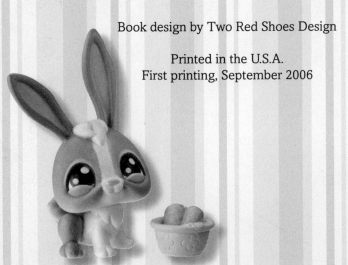

TABLE OF CONTENTS

Whether it's playing catch in the park or running on the beach, these cuddly critters always have the energy to clown around.

SCOTTIE

EYE COLOR: Sky blue

BODY COLOR: White

FAVORITE ACCESSORY:
Tam O'Shanter (Scottish hat)

LIKES: Plaid

DISLIKES: Catty behavior

FAVORITE FOOD: Scotch pie

MOST LIKELY TO SAY: "Has anyone seen my bagpipes?"

FERRET

EYE COLOR: Periwinkle

BODY COLOR: White and charcoal

FAVORITE ACCESSORY:
Pink harness

LIKES: Hiding toys

DISLIKES: Being awake during the day

FAVORITE FOOD: Old shoes

MOST LIKELY TO SAY: "I'm not sneaky . . . I'm just more clever than you are."

HAMSTER

EYE COLOR: Light blue

BODY COLOR: Golden and white

FAVORITE ACCESSORY: Exercise wheel

LIKES: Scampering

DISLIKES: Standing still

FAVORITE FOOD: Corn nibblets

MOST LIKELY TO SAY: "I keep running, even if I never get anywhere."

DALMATIAN

EYE COLOR: Ice blue

BODY COLOR: White with black spots

FAVORITE ACCESSORY: Red bandanna

LIKES: Jumping around the playhouse

DISLIKES: Rainy days

FAVORITE FOOD: Four-alarm chili

MOST LIKELY TO SAY: "Which way to the firehouse?"

MALTESE

EYE COLOR: Turquoise

BODY COLOR: White

FAVORITE ACCESSORY:
Pink wagon

LIKES: People watching

DISLIKES: Hair bows that aren't straight

FAVORITE FOOD:
Cream puffs

MOST LIKELY TO SAY: "Don't hate me for being cuter than you are."

COLLIE

EYE COLOR: Sky blue

BODY COLOR: White and tan

FAVORITE ACCESSORY: Pink race car and helmet

LIKES: Leaving other drivers in the dust

DISLIKES: Traffic

FAVORITE FOOD: Microwave popcorn

MOST LIKELY TO SAY: "Eat my dust!"

BOSTON TERRIER

EYE COLOR: Honey brown

BODY COLOR: Black and white

FAVORITE ACCESSORY: Striped scarf

LIKES: Weekends in the countryside

DISLIKES: Last year's trends

FAVORITE FOOD: Cucumber sandwiches

MOST LIKELY TO SAY: "I'd rather be at the country club."

MALTESE

EYE COLOR: Honey brown

BODY COLOR: Golden brown and white

FAVORITE ACCESSORY: Pink bows

LIKES: Running through obstacle courses

DISLIKES: Waiting for her turn on the swings

FAVORITE FOOD: BBQ chicken

MOST LIKELY TO SAY: "Who wants to race?"

MOUSE

EYE COLOR: Baby blue

BODY COLOR: Gray

FAVORITE ACCESSORY: Earplugs

LIKES: Taking naps in a hammock

DISLIKES: Loud noises

FAVORITE FOOD: Mozzarella cheese

MOST LIKELY TO SAY: "Got anything to nibble on?"

COLLIE

EYE COLOR: Pale blue

BODY COLOR: Golden brown and white

FAVORITE ACCESSORY: Pink carrying case with yellow flowers

LIKES: Socializing

DISLIKES: Being the first one to arrive at a party

FAVORITE FOOD: Peach pie

MOST LIKELY TO SAY: "Can you please pass the gossip column?"

TOTALLY TALENTED

Not only are these pets cute and cuddly, they're also brainy. And since they're quick learners, you'd better be ready to teach them lots of tricks.

HAPPY HAMSTERS

EYE COLOR: Brown

BODY COLOR: Brown and white

FAVORITE ACCESSORY: Skateboard

LIKES: Nibbling on veggies

DISLIKES: Being lazy

FAVORITE FOOD: Radishes

MOST LIKELY TO SAY: "Who's ready for a workout?"

EYE COLOR: Brown

BODY COLOR: Brown and white

FAVORITE ACCESSORY Hamster slide

LIKES: Snacking on potato chips

DISLIKES: Bad cell phone reception

FAVORITE FOOD: Celery with peanut butter

MOST LIKELY TO SAY: "Who wants to go down the slide again?"

EYE COLOR: Light brown

BODY COLOR: Brown and white

FAVORITE ACCESSORY: TV remote control

LIKES: Digging tunnels

DISLIKES: Movies with sad endings

FAVORITE FOOD: Cheese fries

MOST LIKELY TO SAY: "Aren't we the cutest critters?"

BULLDOG

EYE COLOR: Chocolate brown

BODY COLOR: Light brown and white

FAVORITE ACCESSORY: Board games

LIKES: Winning

DISLIKES: Losing

FAVORITE FOOD: T-bone steak

MOST LIKELY TO SAY: "I want a rematch."

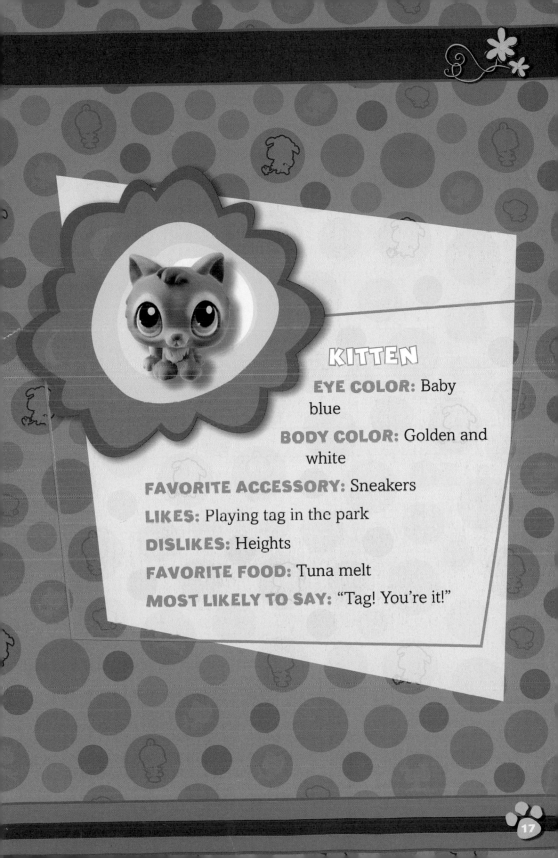

KITTEN

EYE COLOR: Baby blue

BODY COLOR: Golden and white

FAVORITE ACCESSORY: Sneakers

LIKES: Playing tag in the park

DISLIKES: Heights

FAVORITE FOOD: Tuna melt

MOST LIKELY TO SAY: "Tag! You're it!"

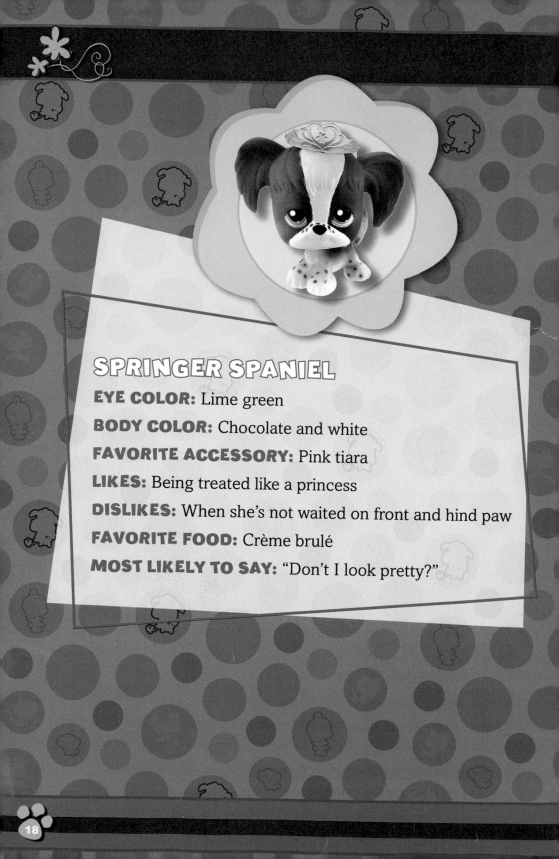

SPRINGER SPANIEL

EYE COLOR: Lime green

BODY COLOR: Chocolate and white

FAVORITE ACCESSORY: Pink tiara

LIKES: Being treated like a princess

DISLIKES: When she's not waited on front and hind paw

FAVORITE FOOD: Crème brulé

MOST LIKELY TO SAY: "Don't I look pretty?"

Whether they're taking a dip in the bathtub or making sure the Doggie Diner is spic-and-span, these pals take getting clean seriously.

GOLDEN RETRIEVER

EYE COLOR: Dusty blue

BODY COLOR: Golden brown

FAVORITE ACCESSORY: Rubber duckie

LIKES: Blowing bubbles

DISLIKES: Dirt

FAVORITE FOOD: PB&J with the crusts cut off

MOST LIKELY TO SAY: "Wanna play fetch?"

BUNNY

EYE COLOR: Purple

BODY COLOR: Golden and white

FAVORITE ACCESSORY: Basket of carrots

LIKES: Hopping through grassy fields

DISLIKES: Having springtime allergies

FAVORITE FOOD: Jelly beans

MOST LIKELY TO SAY: "Hop to it!"

JACK RUSSELL TERRIER

EYE COLOR: Warm brown

BODY COLOR: Golden brown, dark brown, and white

FAVORITE ACCESSORY: Chef's hat

LIKES: Cooking on the grill

DISLIKES: Burnt toast

FAVORITE FOOD: Bacon cheeseburgers

MOST LIKELY TO SAY: "Order's up!"

MOUSE

EYE COLOR: Bright blue

BODY COLOR: White

FAVORITE ACCESSORY: Pink bow

LIKES: Eating crumbs

DISLIKES: Being smaller than everyone else

FAVORITE FOOD: Anything and everything

MOST LIKELY TO SAY: "Can I get that to go in a doggie bag?"

These kitties know how to live it up . . .
and sometimes that means
taking it easy!

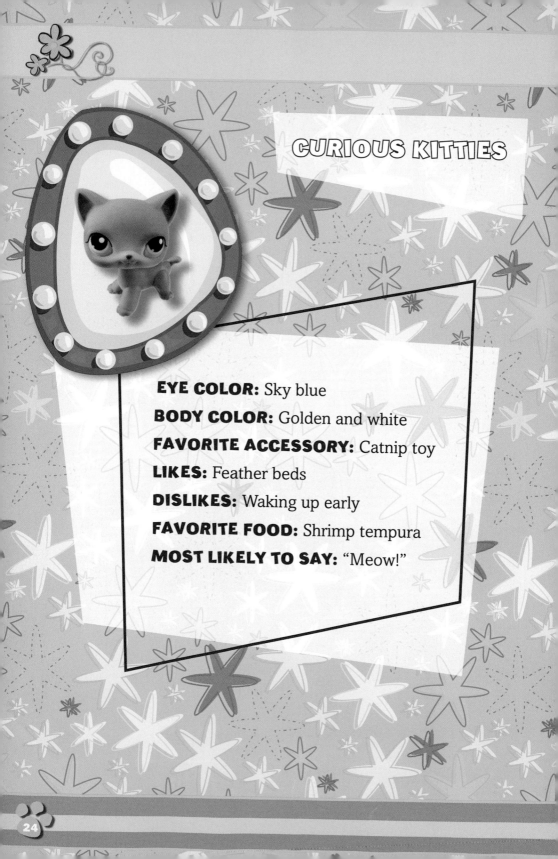

CURIOUS KITTIES

EYE COLOR: Sky blue

BODY COLOR: Golden and white

FAVORITE ACCESSORY: Catnip toy

LIKES: Feather beds

DISLIKES: Waking up early

FAVORITE FOOD: Shrimp tempura

MOST LIKELY TO SAY: "Meow!"

EYE COLOR: Grassy green

BODY COLOR: White and orange

FAVORITE ACCESSORY: Dangling cell phone charm

LIKES: Getting pedicures

DISLIKES: Split ends

FAVORITE FOOD: Salmon sushi

MOST LIKELY TO SAY: "Who wants to go to the salon?"

EYE COLOR: Emerald green

BODY COLOR: Golden and white

FAVORITE ACCESSORY: Sleeping mask

LIKES: Scratching posts

DISLIKES: Hairballs

FAVORITE FOOD: Tuna sushi

MOST LIKELY TO SAY: "Is it time for my cat nap?"

TABBY CAT

EYE COLOR: Yellow-green

BODY COLOR: Golden, white, and dark brown

FAVORITE ACCESSORY: Hairbrush

LIKES: Being pampered

DISLIKES: Swimming

FAVORITE FOOD: Vanilla ice cream

MOST LIKELY TO SAY: "How do I look in this?"

PERSIAN CAT

EYE COLOR: Ice blue

BODY COLOR: Cream, golden, and dark brown

FAVORITE ACCESSORY: Hair ribbon

LIKES: Lazy afternoons spent on the couch

DISLIKES: Aerobics

FAVORITE FOOD: Shrimp cocktail

MOST LIKELY TO SAY: "Would you be a dear and brush out my tangles?"

Break out the suntan lotion—
these little critters are ready to splash
the day away at the beach.

HERMIT CRAB

EYE COLOR: Neon green

BODY COLOR: Pink

FAVORITE ACCESSORY: MP3 player

LIKES: Surfer music

DISLIKES: Big waves

FAVORITE FOOD: Salsa and chips

MOST LIKELY TO SAY: "Catch me if you can. . . ."

IGUANA

EYE COLOR: Orange

BODY COLOR: Light green

FAVORITE ACCESSORY: Sunglasses

LIKES: Lying on sunlit rocks

DISLIKES: Skiing

FAVORITE FOOD: Fruit salad

MOST LIKELY TO SAY: "Reptiles rule!"

You'd better head for a nearby park or swimming pool, because these animals are ready to party. Whatever you do, don't keep these critters cooped up — they love to be out in the sunshine.

BUNNY

EYE COLOR: Aqua

BODY COLOR: White

FAVORITE ACCESSORY: Pink flower

LIKES: Frolicking in gardens

DISLIKES: Good luck charms

FAVORITE FOOD: Carrot cake

MOST LIKELY TO SAY: "Can I have one of your treats?"

GUINEA PIG

EYE COLOR: Dark blue

BODY COLOR: Golden brown and white

FAVORITE ACCESSORY: Jar filled with treats

LIKES: Mystery novels

DISLIKES: Bellyaches

FAVORITE FOOD: Banana bread

MOST LIKELY TO SAY: "Want to cuddle?"

CAT

EYE COLOR: Pale green

BODY COLOR: Orange striped

FAVORITE ACCESSORY
Binoculars

LIKES: Bird-watching

DISLIKES: Cat fights

FAVORITE FOOD: Spaghetti

MOST LIKELY TO SAY: "Can't we all just get along?"

BIRD

EYE COLOR: Dark blue

BODY COLOR: Pale pink

FAVORITE ACCESSORY: Swing

LIKES: Trapeze artists at the circus

DISLIKES: Brussels sprouts

FAVORITE FOOD: Garden salad

MOST LIKELY TO SAY: "Why walk when you can fly?"

CHICK

EYE COLOR: Light blue

BODY COLOR: Yellow

FAVORITE ACCESSORY: Purple basket

LIKES: Hatching ideas

DISLIKES: Heavy metal music

FAVORITE FOOD: Corn muffins

MOST LIKELY TO SAY: "Things are looking up."

BUNNY

EYE COLOR: Light blue

BODY COLOR: White and gray

FAVORITE ACCESSORY: Bubble-gum-flavored lip gloss

LIKES: Hopscotch

DISLIKES: Fences

FAVORITE FOOD: Strawberries and cream

MOST LIKELY TO SAY: "I've got such a sweet tooth."

MOUSE

EYE COLOR: Light purple

BODY COLOR: White

FAVORITE ACCESSORY:
Digital camera

LIKES: Snapping pics of friends

DISLIKES: Painting

FAVORITE FOOD: Cheese fondue

MOST LIKELY TO SAY: "Say 'cheese!'"

CAT

EYE COLOR: Bright green

BODY COLOR: White with gray stripes

FAVORITE ACCESSORY:
Running sneakers

LIKES: Marathons

DISLIKES: Golf

FAVORITE FOOD:
Energy bars

**MOST LIKELY TO
SAY:** "Wanna go for
a run?"

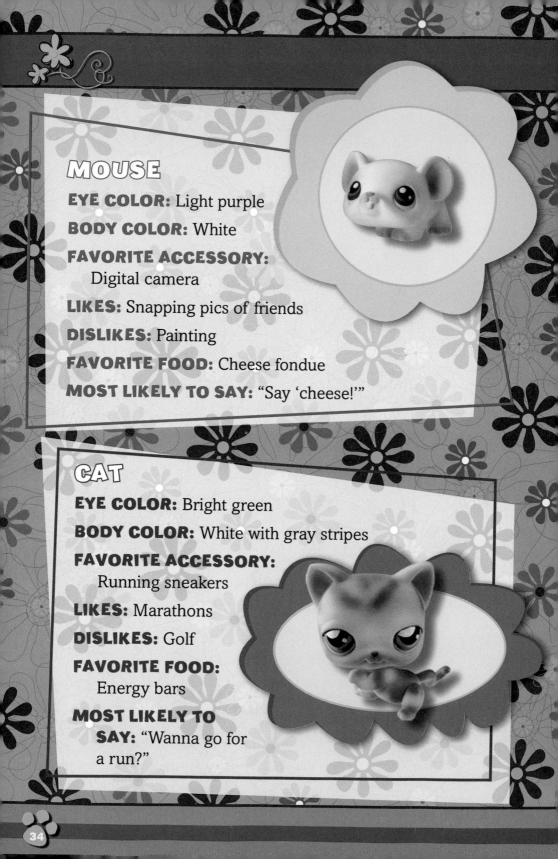

FROG

EYE COLOR: Orange

BODY COLOR: Green and yellow

FAVORITE ACCESSORY: Crown

LIKES: Kissing princesses

DISLIKES: Warts

FAVORITE FOOD: French fries

MOST LIKELY TO SAY: "Pucker up!"

DUCK

EYE COLOR: Light green

BODY COLOR: Yellow

FAVORITE ACCESSORY: Goggles

LIKES: Doing the backstroke

DISLIKES: Getting out of the water

FAVORITE FOOD: Swedish fish

MOST LIKELY TO SAY: "I'm feeling ducky."

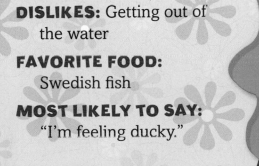

HAMSTER

EYE COLOR: Light blue

BODY COLOR: Golden and white

FAVORITE ACCESSORY: Hamster ball

LIKES: Bowling

DISLIKES: Gutter balls

FAVORITE FOOD: Hot dogs

MOST LIKELY TO SAY: "Striiiike!"

LONG-HAIRED CAT

EYE COLOR: Yellow-green

BODY COLOR: Black and white

FAVORITE ACCESSORY: Box of tissues

LIKES: Sad movies

DISLIKES: Comedies

FAVORITE FOOD: Movie popcorn

MOST LIKELY TO SAY: "Who's up for a movie?"

BEAGLE

EYE COLOR: Apple green

BODY COLOR: Dark chocolate brown

FAVORITE ACCESSORY: Bunny slippers

LIKES: Flannel pajamas

DISLIKES: Snoring

FAVORITE FOOD: Pizza

MOST LIKELY TO SAY: "Who wants to play truth or dare?"

CAT

EYE COLOR: Green-brown

BODY COLOR: Golden

FAVORITE ACCESSORY: Teddy bear

LIKES: Staying up late

DISLIKES: Ghost stories

FAVORITE FOOD: Cheesecake

MOST LIKELY TO SAY: "Will someone braid my ponytail?"

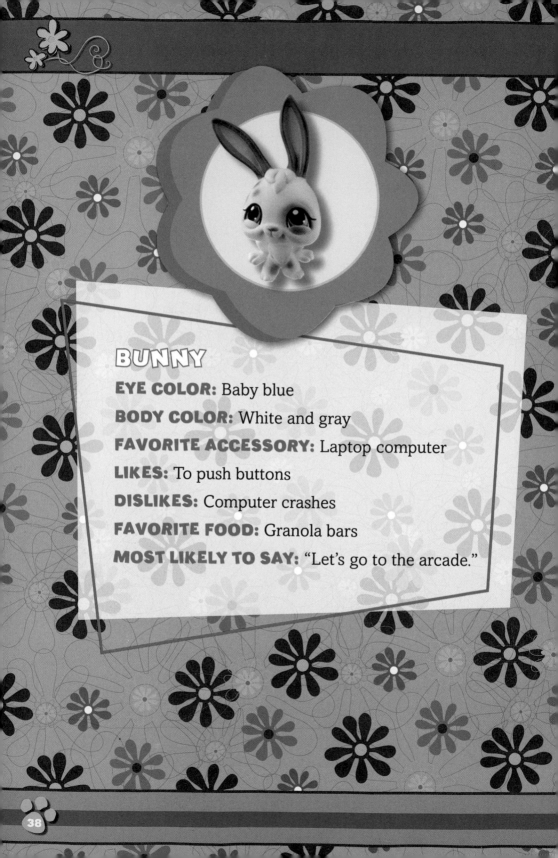

BUNNY

EYE COLOR: Baby blue

BODY COLOR: White and gray

FAVORITE ACCESSORY: Laptop computer

LIKES: To push buttons

DISLIKES: Computer crashes

FAVORITE FOOD: Granola bars

MOST LIKELY TO SAY: "Let's go to the arcade."

SHORTHAIRED CAT

EYE COLOR: Crystal blue

BODY COLOR: White

FAVORITE ACCESSORY: Diary

LIKES: Writing poems

DISLIKES: Salad

FAVORITE FOOD: Mint ice cream

MOST LIKELY TO SAY: "My pen is out of ink again."

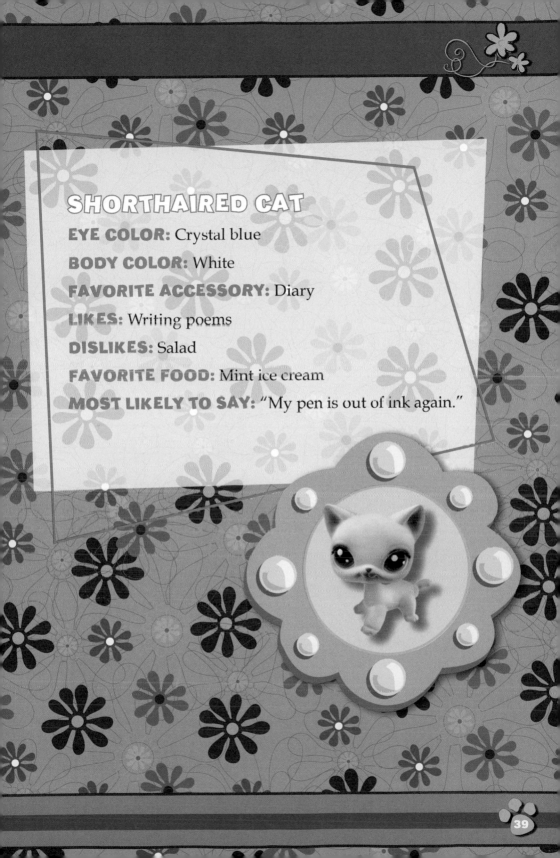

These pretty pets live for shopping. Get your credit card ready, because these critters have a passion for fashion!

SIAMESE CAT

EYE COLOR: Sapphire blue

BODY COLOR: White and charcoal

FAVORITE ACCESSORY: Tiara

LIKES: Anything sparkly

DISLIKES: Not looking her best

FAVORITE FOOD: Caviar

MOST LIKELY TO SAY: "Diamonds are a cat's best friend."

SHIH TZU

EYE COLOR: Dark blue

BODY COLOR: Golden brown and dark brown

FAVORITE ACCESSORY: Hair bow

LIKES: Prancing around

DISLIKES: Disorganized closets

FAVORITE FOOD: Strawberry shortcake

MOST LIKELY TO SAY: "Who wants to go shopping?"

LONG-HAIRED CAT

EYE COLOR: Crystal blue

BODY COLOR: White

FAVORITE ACCESSORY:
Chopsticks

LIKES: Karate

DISLIKES: Using a fork

FAVORITE FOOD: Anything Chinese

MOST LIKELY TO SAY: "Hi-ya!"

FISH

EYE COLOR: Ocean blue

BODY COLOR: Yellow

FAVORITE ACCESSORY: Water

LIKES: Collecting seashells

DISLIKES: Sharks

FAVORITE FOOD:
Seaweed salad

**MOST LIKELY
TO SAY:** "Who wants
to go for a dip?"

PERSIAN CAT

EYE COLOR: Light green

BODY COLOR: White

FAVORITE ACCESSORY: Comfy cat bed

LIKES: Lounging around

DISLIKES: Going to the gym

FAVORITE FOOD: Banana pudding

MOST LIKELY TO SAY: "I'd rather be napping."

LONG-HAIRED CAT

EYE COLOR: Yellow-green

BODY COLOR: Gray

FAVORITE ACCESSORY: Pink carrying case

LIKES: Wearing brightly colored eye shadow

DISLIKES: Homework

FAVORITE FOOD: Sardine sandwiches

MOST LIKELY TO SAY: "Let's go get a makeover."

CALICO CAT

EYE COLOR: Grassy green

BODY COLOR: White, golden, and charcoal

FAVORITE ACCESSORY: Butterfly cat toy

LIKES: Jumping

DISLIKES: Rainy days

FAVORITE FOOD: Cherries

MOST LIKELY TO SAY: "Does my outfit match?"

COCKATOO

EYE COLOR: Pale blue

BODY COLOR: White and yellow

FAVORITE ACCESSORY: Compact mirror

LIKES: Chatting on the phone

DISLIKES: Being away from friends

FAVORITE FOOD: Apple pie

MOST LIKELY TO SAY: "I'm a pretty bird!"

KITTEN

EYE COLOR: Light blue

BODY COLOR: Golden and white

FAVORITE ACCESSORY: Hair dryer

LIKES: Reading gossip magazines

DISLIKES: Nail clippers

FAVORITE FOOD: Salmon teriyaki

MOST LIKELY TO SAY: "Don't I look purrr-fect?"

BLUE BIRD

EYE COLOR: Blue-green

BODY COLOR: Turquoise

FAVORITE ACCESSORY: Perch

LIKES: Getting weekly manicures

DISLIKES: Waiting for salon appointments

FAVORITE FOOD: Sunflower seeds

MOST LIKELY TO SAY: "Can I try a seaweed mud mask?"

POODLE

EYE COLOR: Light blue

BODY COLOR: Light pink

FAVORITE ACCESSORY:
Magic wand

LIKES: Going to the salon for perms

DISLIKES: Frizzy hair

FAVORITE FOOD: Cotton candy

MOST LIKELY TO SAY: "Watch me make this bunny disappear."

BUNNY

EYE COLOR: Light blue

BODY COLOR: Snow white

FAVORITE ACCESSORY:
Magic hat

LIKES: Vanishing

DISLIKES: Reappearing

FAVORITE FOOD:
Carrot muffins

MOST LIKELY TO SAY:
"Now you see me. Now you don't."

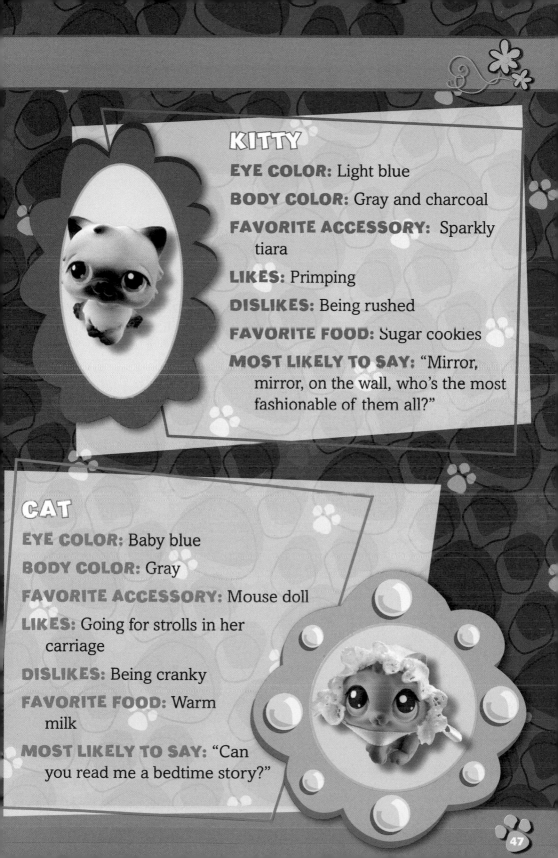

KITTY

EYE COLOR: Light blue

BODY COLOR: Gray and charcoal

FAVORITE ACCESSORY: Sparkly tiara

LIKES: Primping

DISLIKES: Being rushed

FAVORITE FOOD: Sugar cookies

MOST LIKELY TO SAY: "Mirror, mirror, on the wall, who's the most fashionable of them all?"

CAT

EYE COLOR: Baby blue

BODY COLOR: Gray

FAVORITE ACCESSORY: Mouse doll

LIKES: Going for strolls in her carriage

DISLIKES: Being cranky

FAVORITE FOOD: Warm milk

MOST LIKELY TO SAY: "Can you read me a bedtime story?"

When it snows, there's nothing better than having a snowball fight, making snow angels, or staying inside with a mug of hot cocoa. Bundle up . . . winter is here!

POLAR PUPPIES

EYE COLOR: Light blue

BODY COLOR: Gray and white

FAVORITE ACCESSORY: Snowballs

LIKES: Igloos

DISLIKES: Summertime

FAVORITE FOOD: Ice cream

MOST LIKELY TO SAY: "Let's build a snow fort!"

EYE COLOR: Light blue

BODY COLOR: Gray and white

FAVORITE ACCESSORY: Striped scarf

LIKES: Icicles

DISLIKES: Melting ice

FAVORITE FOOD: Frozen bananas

MOST LIKELY TO SAY: "You call this cold?"

EYE COLOR: Baby blue

BODY COLOR: Brown and white

FAVORITE ACCESSORY: Snow shovel

LIKES: Ice fishing

DISLIKES: Not leading the pack

FAVORITE FOOD: Cherry Popsicles

MOST LIKELY TO SAY: "Let's have a snowball fight!"

CAT

EYE COLOR: Sky blue

BODY COLOR: Gray and white

FAVORITE ACCESSORY: Sled

LIKES: Ice-skating

DISLIKES: Cold paws

FAVORITE FOOD: Frozen fish sticks

MOST LIKELY TO SAY: "Have you seen my other mitten?"

BUNNY

EYE COLOR: Arctic blue

BODY COLOR: Golden and white

FAVORITE ACCESSORY: Ear warmers

LIKES: Being bundled up

DISLIKES: Slipping on ice

FAVORITE FOOD: Fruit smoothies

MOST LIKELY TO SAY: "Who wants to build a snow bunny?"

ST. BERNARD

EYE COLOR: Ocean blue

BODY COLOR: Honey brown and white

FAVORITE ACCESSORY: Earmuffs

LIKES: Snuggling

DISLIKES: Getting lost

FAVORITE FOOD: Oatmeal cookies

MOST LIKELY TO SAY: "I'll rescue you if you fall!"

DOG DAYS

There won't be any cat fights here . . . this is a dogs-only party. There's plenty of kibble and squeaky toys for everyone, so come on over!

BEAGLE

EYE COLOR: Honey brown

BODY COLOR: Golden brown

FAVORITE ACCESSORY: Teddy bear

LIKES: Being spoiled

DISLIKES: Cooking

FAVORITE FOOD: Anything "takeout"

MOST LIKELY TO SAY: "Heard any good gossip?"

POODLE

EYE COLOR: Pale blue

BODY COLOR: White

FAVORITE ACCESSORY: Flower hair clip

LIKES: Hugs and kisses

DISLIKES: Rude behavior

FAVORITE FOOD: French toast

MOST LIKELY TO SAY: *"Bonjour!"*

CHIHUAHUA

EYE COLOR: Chocolate brown

BODY COLOR: Cream and light brown

FAVORITE ACCESSORY: Chew toy

LIKES: Trips to Mexico

DISLIKES: Almost being stepped on

FAVORITE FOOD: Burritos

MOST LIKELY TO SAY: "Can I borrow your sweater?"

PUG

EYE COLOR: Brown-green

BODY COLOR: Light and dark brown

FAVORITE ACCESSORY: Romance novels

LIKES: Long walks on the beach

DISLIKES: Stormy weather

FAVORITE FOOD: Anything by candlelight

MOST LIKELY TO SAY: "I'm such a romantic."

SCOTTIE

EYE COLOR: Emerald green

BODY COLOR: Black

FAVORITE ACCESSORY:
Fashion magazines

LIKES: Reading the style section
of the newspaper

DISLIKES: Wearing plaid and stripes

FAVORITE FOOD: Cappuccino

MOST LIKELY TO SAY: "I've got my stylist on speed dial."

BOXER

EYE COLOR: Honey brown

BODY COLOR: White and
brown

FAVORITE ACCESSORY:
Fire hydrant toy

LIKES: Going for walks
around the neighborhood

DISLIKES: Bad attitudes

FAVORITE FOOD: Anything that can be shared

MOST LIKELY TO SAY: "Let's be friends."

COCKER SPANIEL

EYE COLOR: Warm brown

BODY COLOR: Cream and golden

FAVORITE ACCESSORY: Purple tiara

LIKES: Singing in the shower

DISLIKES: Being off-key

FAVORITE FOOD: Hot tea with lemon

MOST LIKELY TO SAY: "I should have been a professional singer."

GERMAN SHEPHERD

EYE COLOR: Light brown

BODY COLOR: Golden brown

FAVORITE ACCESSORY: Flashlight

LIKES: Staying up late

DISLIKES: Strangers

FAVORITE FOOD: Strong coffee

MOST LIKELY TO SAY: "I'll protect you!"

EYE COLOR: Lavender

BODY COLOR: Cocoa brown and white

FAVORITE ACCESSORY: Anything that can be fetched

LIKES: Running around with friends

DISLIKES: Being alone

FAVORITE FOOD: Peanut butter and banana sandwiches

MOST LIKELY TO SAY: "Let's go to the dog park."

EYE COLOR: Lavender

BODY COLOR: Golden brown and white

FAVORITE ACCESSORY: The telephone

LIKES: Telling jokes

DISLIKES: Being told to be quiet

FAVORITE FOOD: Chicken nuggets

MOST LIKELY TO SAY: "Did you hear the one about . . ."

EYE COLOR: Lavender

BODY COLOR: Cocoa brown

FAVORITE ACCESSORY: A cozy blanket

LIKES: Taking naps

DISLIKES: Alarm clocks

FAVORITE FOOD: Herbal tea

MOST LIKELY TO SAY: "I'm just gonna take a quick cat nap."

Think you're seeing double?
These twins are the luckiest pets around —
they've got their best friend with them
all the time. And it doesn't hurt that
they love the same things, too.

TWIN KITTENS

EYE COLOR: Bright blue

BODY COLOR: White

EYE COLOR: Sky blue

BODY COLOR: White and orange

FAVORITE ACCESSORIES: Each other

LIKE: Cuddling

DISLIKE: Water fights

FAVORITE FOOD: Sardines

MOST LIKELY TO SAY: "We need a good home!"

TWIN TURTLES

EYE COLOR: Brown

BODY COLOR: Green with spotted shells

EYE COLOR: Brown

BODY COLOR: Green with brown shell and pink spots

FAVORITE ACCESSORIES: Suave sunglasses

LIKE: Moving slowly

DISLIKE: Minimum speed limits

FAVORITE FOOD: Molasses

MOST LIKELY TO SAY: "Are we there yet?"

TWIN MONKEYS

EYE COLOR: Purple

BODY COLOR: Golden and brown

EYE COLOR: Jungle green

BODY COLOR: Tan and cocoa

FAVORITE ACCESSORIES: Vines to swing from

LIKE: Swinging

DISLIKE: Being separated

FAVORITE FOOD: Banana split (with two spoons)

MOST LIKELY TO SAY: "Wanna hang out?"

How big is your Littlest Pet Shop™?
Check out the first 80 pets!

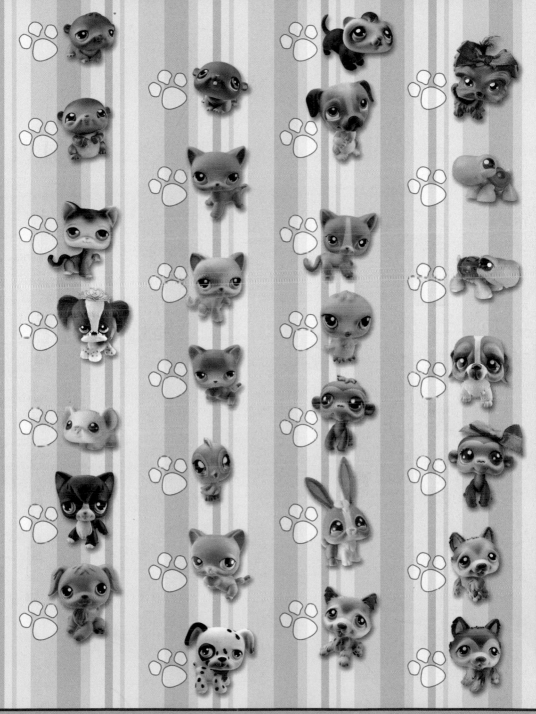